Girl, You're Amazing!

WRITTEN BY Virginia Kroll

ILLUSTRATED BY Mélisande Potter

Albert Whitman & Company
Morton Grove, Illinois

For Nancy Furstinger and all my other sisters
of the pen—girls, you're amazing! —V. K.

To Mama and Daddy, and to my daughters,
Giselle and Chloë. —M. P.

Library of Congress Cataloging-in-Publication Data

Kroll, Virginia L.
Girl, you're amazing! / by Virginia L. Kroll ; illustrated by Mélisande Potter.
p. cm.
Summary: Rhyming text celebrates the many remarkable things that girls can achieve,
from packing a lunchbox and lacing their shoes to swishing a basketball and climbing a tree.
ISBN 0-8075-2930-3
[1. Sex Role—Fiction. 2. Stories in Rhyme.] I. Potter, Mélisande, ill. II. Title.
PZ8.3.K8997 Gi 2001 [E]—dc21 00-010207

The illustrations are mixed media
(including watercolor and gouache) on paper.
The typeface is Gararond.
The design is by Scott Piehl.

Girl, you're amazing, the things you can do!

Pack your own lunchbox and lace your own shoe,

build sandy castles or sketch summer scenes,

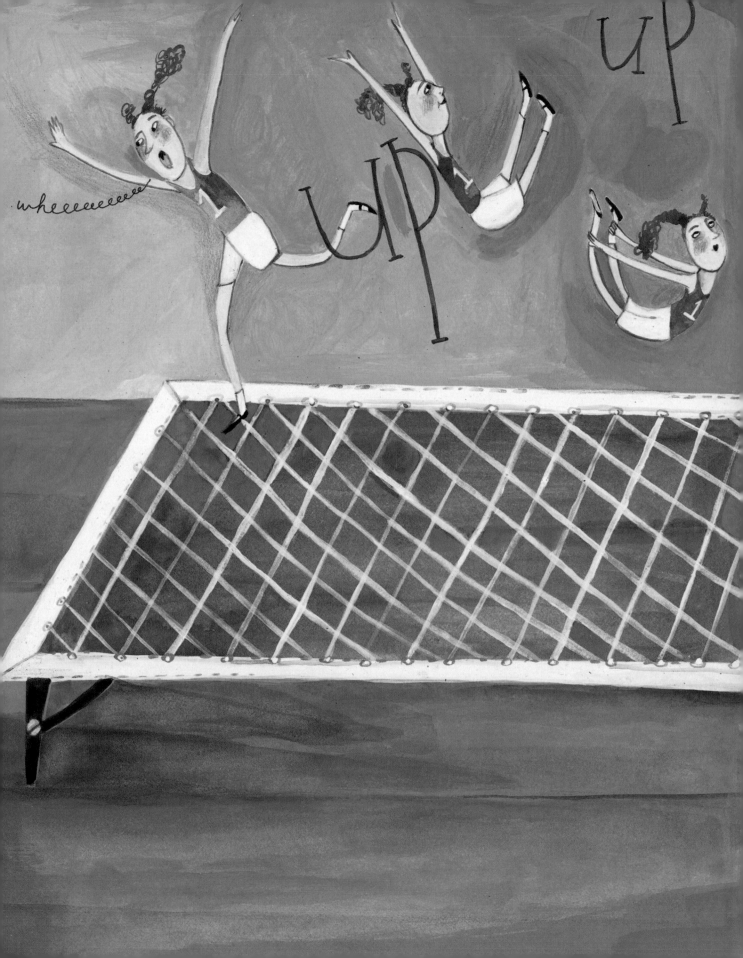

jump higher, highest on taut trampolines.

How to write stories where fantasies grow,
when to pick pumpkins and how to fly kites,
just where to search for the sky's satellites.

Girl, you're amazing, the art you create!

T-shirts in tie-dye, a Mother's Day plate,
bright city chalk-walks, piñatas of clay,
neat origami and paper-mâché.

Girl, you're amazing, the show you put on!

Playing that saxophone, twirling baton,
strumming and drumming in time to the beat,
dancing and swirling with light-as-air feet.

Girl, you're amazing, the help that you lend!

Loaning lunch money—again—to your friend,
helping your brother with math he finds tough,
seeing the puppies are fed just enough.

Girl, you're amazing, the sport you can be!

Swishing that basketball, climbing a tree,

spiking that volleyball, striking ten pins,

shaking hands after the other team wins.

Girl, you're amazing, the love that you show!

Braiding your cousin's hair, row after row,
making a sweet "get well" card for your niece,
reading to Great-Grandpa, praying for peace.

Girl, you're amazing, the things that you are!

Great babysitter and spelling bee star,

poet, computer whiz, food drive director,
animal lover and wildlife protector,

daughter and grandchild,

sister and chum.

Think of it too, Girl, the things you'll become!

Grace, Emma, Jess, Amy, Chelsea, Christine, Cheryl, Dawn, Geetha, Kim, Rachel, Maureen, Wendy, Sophia, Nicole, Abby, Mel, Sara, Rose, Faith, Frieda, Jane, Isabel, Hannah, Olivia, Katya, Pam, Becca, Masami, Barb, Mia, Jo, Sam . . .

Steph, Heather, Paige, Alex, Mandy, Renée,
Jen, Doli, Trish, Phyllis, Carole, Ruth, Kay,
Ashley, Karima, Liz, Mary, Brooke, Ann,
Nancy, Val, Quinn, Karen, Chi-Wei, Meg, Fran,
Natalie, Ellen, Eve, Marge, Lisa, Sue—

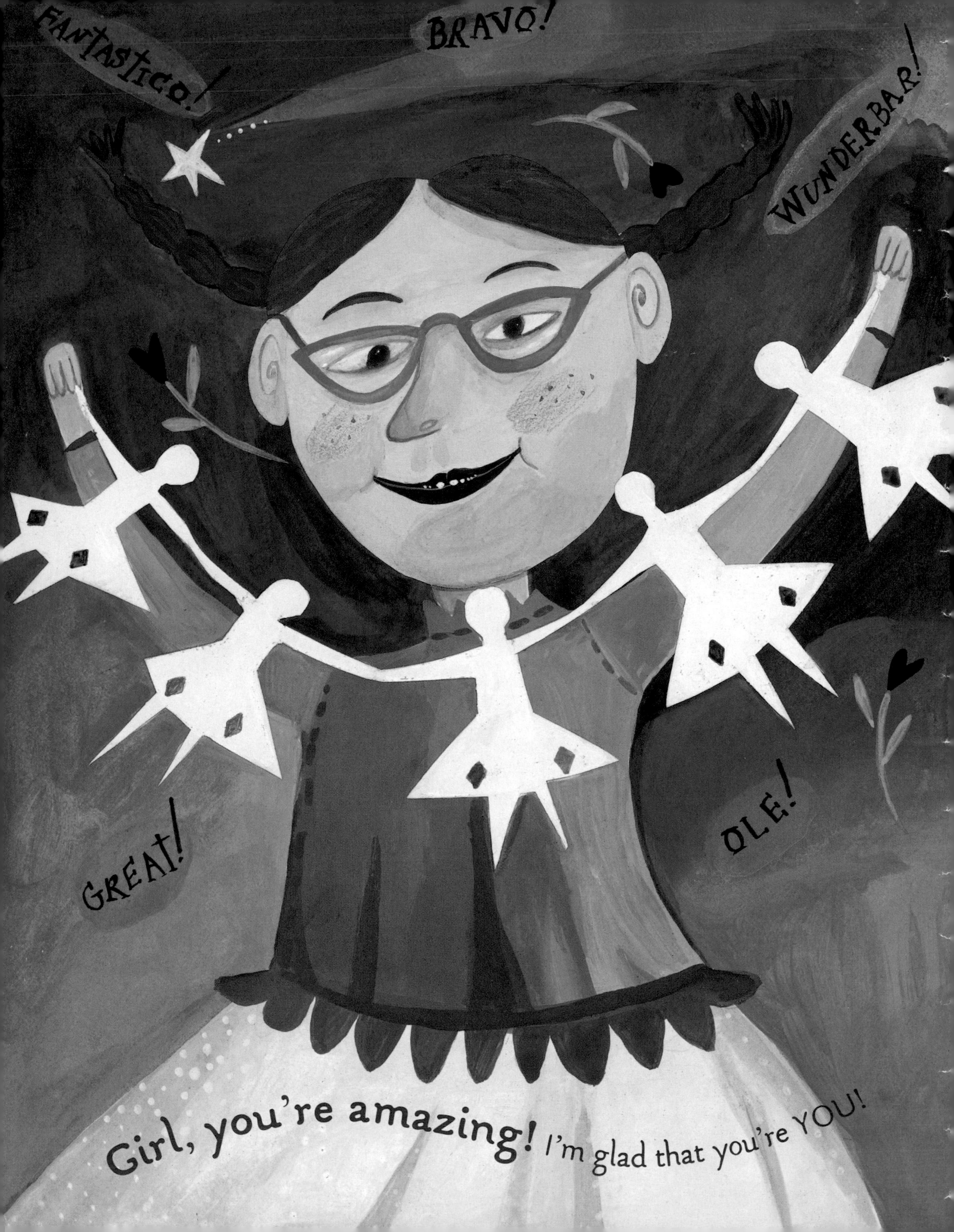

Girl, you're amazing! I'm glad that you're YOU!